1961

GE... ...
Gu... ...
The ... ...

W9-ABG-675

3 0301 00033779 6

ALBRECHT GOES

The
Burnt Offering

TRANSLATED BY
MICHAEL HAMBURGER

PANTHEON

LIBRARY
College of St. Francis
JOLIET, ILL.

COPYRIGHT © 1956 BY PANTHEON BOOKS INC.
333 SIXTH AVENUE, NEW YORK 14, NEW YORK

TITLE OF ORIGINAL GERMAN EDITION
DAS BRANDOPFER
S. FISCHER VERLAG, FRANKFURT/MAIN

LIBRARY OF CONGRESS CATALOG CARD NUMBER:
56-6015
MANUFACTURED IN THE U.S.A.

833.9
G598

8-18-61 Pearson Information Center $2.50 g

31473

THE BURNT OFFERING

THESE PAGES EVOKE THINGS PAST. BUT TO what end? Not to perpetuate hatred. Only to raise up a sign in obedience to the eternal sign which commands: "Thus far and no further." A commemorative sign inscribed—on what and for whom? Oh, he writes on air who remembers them, them whose earthly part has passed away, dust and ashes in the earth and wind. Men have forgotten. And indeed one must forget, for how could one go on living if one could not forget? Yet at times there is need of one who remembers. For this is more than ashes in the wind. This is a flame. The world

7

would freeze to death if it were not for this
flame.

If it hadn't been for that business with the
baby carriage, coming on top of everything,
I don't think I should have done it. Human
beings are so unfeeling, sir, more unfeeling
than cattle. Take any beast—I know how a
beast takes notice when one of its mates is
getting the knife—I had to go out to the
slaughterhouse often enough when my husband was away with the army. Yes, dumb
creatures take notice all right. But as for
us, we say, things like that oughtn't to be
allowed to happen; or we say, but this is
terrible, and then we get used to it. And in
the business they also say, clients are clients
and good money is good money. And besides, I never really knew anything about
the Jews; in these parts there were only two
families, Dr. Rosenbaum's at No. 12, just

on the other side of the road, but they went off to Holland as soon as Hitler came to power; his profession was something like yours, sir, he was a head librarian, I think —those Rosenbaums and that little Miss Wolf, but she'd started keeping her own company by then, and that's why it took them so long to find out she'd turned on the gas . . . it was getting on toward 1938. No, I can't say I knew anything about them; I don't say that to excuse myself, it wouldn't excuse very much in any case, we should have taken more trouble to find out, I know, at least I know it now. As for the new lords and masters, I didn't have much respect for them. They came rattling in to buy a quarter of liver sausage or cold cuts, I wrapped it up for them and said: "Good day." And my husband said, "Heil Hitler!" So we sometimes had words over this. "Now you've done it again," my husband said, "not using the proper form of greeting. And that was the Kreisleiter's lady in person." So I said, "And who might that be, the

9

Kreisleiter's lady in person?" "Don't get
too big for your boots," my husband said
then, "Dachau is not as far away as you
think." So I asked, "Dachau—what's that?"
Yes, sir, that's what I asked him, for I
really didn't know, and that was as late as
'35 or '36. Then my husband said, "Dachau
—that's something you won't find in your
prayer book." So I kept quiet and asked no
more questions.

That's how it was in the first few years.
Till the day—it was in December '38, I remember the day quite well, it was a very
cold day—when the very first woman came
in wearing the yellow star on her coat. She
came in just when the lunch hour was over,
and I was alone in the shop. "Half a pound
of beef, please," she said, keeping an eye on
the door all the time, as if someone were
after her. "Do you want it on the bone?" I
asked her, as I always do, and then I saw
the star on her coat, very neatly sewn on
with yellow thread it was, strong enough to
last her a lifetime. "Yes, please, on the

bone," she said. And I get it ready for her, she pays for it, says "Good afternoon" and leaves the shop. But in the evening—I remember this too as if it had happened yesterday—my husband had put away the paper and was fiddling about with the radio, I asked him, "What really went on the other day at the synagogue, and why couldn't you put out the fire?" At that time he was serving in the auxiliary fire service, and they'd got the alarm that night in November. "That's simple," my husband said, "when we'd never fixed the hose to the hydrant." "And why not?" I asked. "Why not," my husband said, and his face turned as white as a sheet, "you shouldn't ask too many questions. Don't worry your head, Greta," he went on, "all that's over and done with."

But by that time I'd already got up and gone out the door, and—without troubling to put on a coat—I went out and walked all around our part of the town, for an hour or more. I could see lights in St. Peter's Church—it was still standing then—so I

stood on the steps for a moment and listened
to the singing, and then I knew how things
would turn out, just as they did turn out six
years later, almost to the very day. "Is that
how you went out?" my husband asked when
I got back, "without so much as a scarf
round your neck? You can catch your death
that way!" And I said, "That's right, my
death."

The war started and my husband had to
leave at once, on the second day. It had done
him no good to join the Party just before,
and when he told them at the recruiting center that being a butcher was a vital occupa-
tion, they said to him, "Yes, but you've got
a wife to look after the business, and she
knows her job." All the same he was dis-
charged again, just after the Polish cam-
paign, only they got him back in February,
1940, and from then on I was all alone here
till fall 1947—he was a prisoner of war till

then. The first months of the war—everyone
was very busy then, there were so many reg-
ulations, and you had to keep them all in
your head; I must have spent two evenings
every week just sticking on the ration-card
coupons. There wasn't any time to sit back
and think about things, and I was almost
glad there wasn't. There were customers
who said things like this: "Just you wait,
they'll soon give you a fine butcher's shop
in Paris or London. Believe me, by the tenth
of October we'll be in London, my brother
got it straight from headquarters." I never
said a word in answer to such foolish talk,
only looked up at St. Peter's sometimes, you
could just see the tip of the spire through
the big shop window, and then I thought to
myself: how long?

And then—the day when two men from
the political department came in, two young
louts I should say, golden pheasants is what
they called their sort; people were always
inventing funny nicknames like that, but
they shouldn't have done . . . well, those fel-

lows produced a sheet of paper. "Gauleiter's orders," they said. A Gauleiter, you probably still remember, was someone very much like the Lord God Almighty in those days. "What about?" I asked, and had a nasty taste in my mouth. "You have been selected for a very special task, Frau Walker," one of them began, and the other: "And this special task requires a very special kind of political tact, you might say." I hadn't the faintest idea what they wanted me to do. "Well, what is it, then?" I asked. "You're going to be the Jews' butcher," one of them said now—I can still see him standing there, a great fat lout with yellow horn-rimmed glasses, not thirty years old, and the other screamed like an echo, "The Jews' butcher," and then they burst out laughing as if they'd told me a particularly good joke: "The Jews' butcher, the Jews' butcher," and just couldn't stop themselves. At last they told me the rest: from now on all the Jews in the town would only be allowed to buy their meat in my shop, and on Fridays, every

Friday afternoon between five and seven, my shop would be kept open for the "non-Aryan population," as they called it. "You will prove yourself worthy of this trust." That sounded like a threat and was probably meant that way. The two louts brought out their cigarette cases, sniffed about a bit, threw a few more silly remarks at me ("Don't think you're going to feed Abraham and Sarah veal cutlets and steaks") and took off.

The next day this sinister bit of news appeared in a list of local instructions, and the day after it was the topic of all my customers' conversation. Here I must say there were quite a few of them who didn't like this order and who just looked embarrassed when others talked about it. Some even made no bones about saying what they thought of it. "I only wonder what all this will lead to," one woman might say; and another: "Something pretty bad, you can be sure." "As sure as you're standing here," a third one joined in. But then suddenly some-

15

body called out, I don't remember if it was
a man or a woman: "Only be sure you give
the place a good airing on Fridays, or no
Christian will be able to stand it the next
day, Frau Walker." And a young woman—
I remember her all right, sir—perked up:
"My husband's just home on leave, he'd like
to know whether you wouldn't like him to
lend you his gas mask for next Friday
night." Well, if I wasn't wise till then to
what was brewing up, I certainly had a good
idea now.

On Friday between one and five my shop
was to be closed—this, too, was printed on
the instruction sheet, and I still know very
well what I felt like that first Friday afternoon. Immediately after closing the shop at
one I'd given the stone floor a good washing;
I couldn't touch my food that day, but I
felt like having a nap. Well, you know that
life sometimes does you a good turn, and
you doze off in the midst of your terrors. I
really did go to sleep, but it was a sleep full
of bad dreams. I don't want to talk about it,

dreams are only dreams and what came later was worse than any dream. Anyway, that's how I spent the hours before opening time. Shortly before five I'd unlocked the door again, I didn't want to keep them waiting outside; but it was a quarter past five before the first customers turned up. I dare say they'd already had some dealings with my other customers and wanted to make sure of not meeting anyone here. Well, that evening I had my first taste of all the things one could experience in my new work: the timid way in which they handed me their ration cards across the counter, those little colored rags of paper, a different color each month, but every month the same big "J" was printed on them, the same impudent "J" that stood for "Jew," and what they could buy for those cards wasn't enough from the very start to keep body and soul together. Of course they didn't know me, and so they followed every movement of my scissors mistrustfully as I cut out the week's coupons. Later I understood all this. Their fear

17

and their mistrust. And I understood why some of them were so tired that they had to hold on to the counter. For they'd had to walk for an hour or two to get to my shop, they'd been forbidden to use the trams and on the seats in the Schlosspark there were notices saying: "Not for Jews." Some of them were in a great hurry, I was soon struck by that, but the reason for this too didn't become clear to me till much later: on Friday evenings at six o'clock their Sabbath begins, and an orthodox Jew doesn't like to go about his worldly business at that hour or to be out and on the move. They had chosen that day and shopping hour for the Jews so as to spoil the beginning of their Sabbath for them; I understood this in time, they took good care to make me understand.

For already on the third or fourth Friday I had visitors. Supervision? Supervision isn't really the right word, for they paid hardly any attention to me, at least that's how it seemed. They came in twos or threes, in uniform. They carried a Bible about with them,

18

a real showpiece of a Bible it was, large and heavy. Then they struck a great pose, as though they were going to deliver a sermon, opened the Bible and started declaiming. Not a word of what's in the Bible, mind you, but evil rhymes and verses. "Sow's meat . . ." no, I can't repeat what they said—no, sir, I simply can't. But I still know every one of those verses, that I do. You're surprised that I still know them, are you? No, you're not surprised. Can anyone forget such things? How they stood there, "what a fine fellow I am," was their attitude, young, fair-haired lads, quite good-looking, you know the type—and beside them the others, not much to look at they were, the women with their shopping bags made of pressed paper, their clothes all shabby, and the men not much better, and all of them as if they felt a whip on their backs, but faces—real faces. . . . Just a moment, sir, excuse me a moment, please.

19

It is time for me to inform you who is speaking here and who I am myself, the man who is listening to it. Well, as far as I am concerned, the introduction will not take me very long. I am an assistant in the Museum Library and live out here in the garden city, in a corner house. I occupy a room on the third floor of that house, a house, by the way, which has only recently been put up again, and the room is a very pleasant one. The woman who faces me, my informant— she herself has mentioned her name already —is Frau Walker, the wife of the butcher and landlord, Karl Walker. As to how it came about that I am listening to her account—and this part of an account can hardly be left unfinished at the point she had reached—this will take a little longer to explain. How does one get to know a story?

20

By being inquisitive. All right, but I don't happen to be inquisitive. Or one gets to know a story if one is concerned with the human lot—anyone's lot, or a certain person's. But is the human lot the concern of an assistant in a museum library? Manuscripts, *incunabula,* facsimiles, first editions—these, it goes without saying, interest him. But no; I say that the human lot is our concern. One isn't a sub-tenant in the house of Frau Walker, the woman with the burn on her face, without asking oneself what sort of a person she is, and what sort of lot was cast for her. One doesn't only walk through her shop on coming home, stopping to buy some tongue or ham for one's supper. If Karl Walker is there, well, in that case it might be enough to exchange those words which are always ready on everyone's lips, which no one need trouble to search for: "Good evening . . . pretty hot today . . . getting cooler, don't you think. . . . Had a hard day, sir? . . . What would you like tonight?"

Strange: how does this man come to have

this particular wife? Or, still more strange:
how does this woman come to have this particular husband? A butcher—but does a
butcher look like him? There's something
depleted, flattened out, about the man, rather
as if history had run over him like a tractor,
leaving nothing but a pair of watery blue
eyes and a heavy, weary mouth. ("Good
day. What can I do for you, miss? Pork
sausages—yes, they're quite fresh, in today.
Very best quality, none better anywhere.")
But who is that woman who helps in the
shop at the busiest times, between nine and
half past ten in the mornings, and after five
in the evenings? At those times the sale of
meat and the sale of sausages are separate
and the woman stands on the sausage side,
if one may put it like that, also acting as
cashier. Anyone can see that her hands were
not made for the butcher's knife; as for her
great dark eyes, what they were intended for
is a different question. Her mouth, a severe,
a—I know no better word—a tell-no-secrets
mouth, will give nothing away. Yet there

can be no doubt: it is she who is in charge, responsible here. I remember it well: when I inquired about the room in reply to an advertisement and asked Herr Walker about it—it was some time in the early afternoon and I found no one there but the man, a short, rather stocky man in a striped butcher's jacket, black and white—I was told, "You'd better talk to the lady," and I remember how this "with the lady" struck me: this was just how an elderly shop assistant speaks about his female employer, and later events confirmed my first impression. So I went to see the lady, a little apprehensive from the first (why, I wonder?), opened the door which Herr Walker had indicated and came to a room—it adjoined the shop—half office, half living room: there I found Frau Walker, busy with her typewriter. She listened to my request, gave my face a searching, unsmiling look—it was like a test—and led me to the room. It was a room on the third floor, bright and with a pleasant view. The furniture—a couch, a wardrobe, a table, a washstand and chairs—was of light natural wood and obviously quite new. What struck me was the absence of little embroidered or crochet-work mats, of family portraits on the walls and other suburban horrors of that kind; instead, there was a reading lamp of the latest design and, as the sole ornament on the wall, an excellent reproduction of Rembrandt's *Tobias*. "I should think you'll prefer to put in other things to suit your own taste," Frau Walker said, and as she said it I decided then and there to take the room.

Once again: who is this woman? If it was my task to find an answer to this question— as, indeed, it is for question and answer that we come up against one another on our way —she did nothing to facilitate this task, nothing, or next to nothing. We rarely had occasion to exchange more than a word of greeting; I did not come face to face with her every day—far from it, as I did not particularly like coming in through the shop. Rather, it had happened once or twice that neighbors tried to draw me into conversation and showed an unmistakable desire to find out something about my landlady. In fact—as I now recall—it was not in Frau Walker's account that I first heard the words "Jew's butcher." *"Where* did you say you live?" somebody asked me the other day, half incredulously, half inquisitorially, and, when I told him, retorted, "Oh, I see, in the Jews' butcher's house"; but then, without giving me time to question him in my turn, he asked again, "And Frau Walker —how is she doing these days?" Whereupon—what else could I do—I put an end to the conversation with some noncommittal remark and took my leave. This woman and her past—what was her past?—this is not a topic to be discussed over the garden wall, as one knows well enough without knowing how one came to know it.

The next thing—I am trying to remember the sequence of events—was our meeting one evening at the "Pro Israel" Society, an association that has made it its business to

31473

LIBRARY
College of St. Francis
JOLIET, ILL.

prepare the ground for the renewal of genuine relations with Israel. A colleague at the
library had introduced me to it, and I was
not a little astonished when I discovered my
landlady among those taking part in the
small gathering, not, indeed, as an occasional
guest, as I could see at once, but as a well-
informed member. In the room itself we
could only exchange a silent greeting, but it
so happened that we walked home together
and that our conversation returned to the
evening's discussions. "Speak ye comfort-
ably to Jerusalem!" I took up the speaker's
motto again and said, "But that, of course,
is not so easy . . . I am thinking of the young
generation in our country, to whom one
would like to be of some use. They hardly
have such a thing as convictions or a point
of view any more, and to love ideas for their
own sake is very hard indeed." Frau Walker
replied, "Even so, a few of the exiles have
returned, so we should make those few aware
of how we feel about them. And anyway, if
only one or two of us remain alive to the

meaning of the terror, this too will not be in
vain." As she said this, I looked at her side-
ways and could clearly see that she was talking about a terror that was wholly alive in
her: the terror, the state of being terrified
by everything of which human beings are
capable. I was on the point of asking her
how she had come to join this "Pro Israel"
Society, but it isn't so easy to ask Frau
Walker anything. Besides, we were almost
back at the house. My landlady unlatched
the door, we said good night in the hallway.
Since then a fortnight has passed, and no
other encounter offered itself.

But today . . . I walk into the sitting room,
my glance, like the glance of every man in
my profession, runs along the bookcase and
is caught by a Hebrew title on the spine of
one book. A book in Hebrew? Well, there
I'm on my own ground, so I can touch the
book without being thought impertinent and
ask her: "How did that book come your
way?" "That's a long story," she said, but
there must have been something in my

glance, something quite different from mere curiosity, that made her add: "I'll tell it to you one day." Then I said—it was in the evening, we were standing beside her chest of drawers, one could hear the silence of the house like a voice beyond time—and I said, "Now."

And so she began to tell her story, or rather to evoke it from the depths. That is not to say that what followed now ("If it hadn't been for that business with the baby carriage . . .") poured out of her like a waterfall. No, it would be truer to say that she hauled it up out of a deep shaft. She told her story slowly and with long pauses. Waterfall or shaft—no matter; she was speaking, and it was not fitting to interrupt her while she spoke. As long as she was silent, I heard the clock ticking, time steadily passing. Time that is grace and judgment. Already judgment. Still grace.

"Just a moment, sir, excuse me a moment, please," she had said then and left the room. Not a sound had reached me from the world outside, as no sound would reach one down in a mine. Somebody must have come in, Herr Walker or a visitor. Now she returned, dressed to go out, a Red Cross bag in her hand. "I have to leave quickly for a neighbor's house," she said, "they've had an accident, a child scalded its arm. That's a kind of relic of the war years, I mean being called in for cases of that sort," she added with a faint smile.

She was right back in the present and her thoughts, most probably, were already occupied with the child. Our conversation had been broken off. Conversation, I suppose, is the wrong word; she had done the talking, but if listening is a different form of speaking, it was a conversation indeed. She hadn't said: "I'll be back in no time, please wait here." Nor had she said, what she could easily have said: "That will have to be all for now; more another day." But the opening sentence of her account was something to which I could go back myself, something like a promise of a sequel to her story. Not a pleasant story—that much is certain even now. But, then, who says that one cannot draw some light from a gloomy story, as one strikes bright fire from dark stone?

A T ONCE, I SAID TO MYSELF, I MUST HEAR
the end of the story at once. Even for
Frau Walker's sake I mustn't delay it too
long. A person who has the courage to ex-
pose such experiences to the light of day,
once they are safely buried, opens up, like
the body of a woman in childbirth. Soon the
trap door must close again. But not until
someone has been let into the secret. I was
that person.

Our conversation had taken place on a
Tuesday; on Wednesday and Thursday
nights I had professional engagements and
I could no longer cancel my acceptance of
an invitation for Friday night. There were
eleven of us in the house of a County Court
judge, the buffet supper was excellent and

so was the dry Moselle wine, we had chamber music, a sprightly trio by a French com-
poser of the seventeenth century, a flute
sonata by Couperin and something by
Mozart at the end; there was the good conversation of open-minded persons in which
I should have taken part with pleasure at
any other time—but how could I enjoy a
ham sandwich when my ears buzzed with
"Half a pound of beef, please!" and what
does Mozart sound like on this devastated
earth ("You are going to be the Jews'
butcher!")? Also I wasn't interested in hearing the County Court judge's opinions
on Byzantine mosaics—I wanted to know
whether he had punished one of those who
set fire to the synagogue, or would have
punished him, I should probably say.

A fever was creeping over me, I could
feel it now in my spine, now on my temples;
I took my leave early, went home and en-
dured the long night as best I could. At last
it was day and I knew at once that it would
turn into one of those days on which one's

life and destiny get more deeply under one's
skin than on other days. A fever has eaten
away some of our power of resistance, we
cannot choose among the things that happen
to us, but just for that reason such days are
rarely insignificant or a mere waste of time.
The house in which we live and which often
enough is nothing more to us than so many
floors piled one above the other, so many instructions and prohibitions ("Don't leave
the light on all night," "Kindly wipe your
shoes," "Shut the door after you, please"),
nothing more than a conglomeration of letter boxes and milk bottles—suddenly it is
the house of destiny, life leaps at me from
every door, a panther, an enemy, an ally, a
life that I love—as ever. Everyone who lives
there concerns me, I share life with them all,
I am their companion, their friend; the
breath they draw affects me, my heartbeat
responds to theirs. We are no longer divided
by that wall, and what at other times is simply a source of irritation or worse—the sound
of electric switches next door, the sighs, the

thumps and shouts, the conflict of words, the message of their love-hate—all expressions of the life of the young couple, musicians both of them, who share the third floor with me—suddenly all this affects me differently: the inexpressible gravity with which the life of strangers touches upon one's own pervades everything. Suddenly the girl accountant on the first floor is no longer the rather pert occupant of number 5, but that which in truth she is at every hour, whether she knows it or not: a life that seeks fulfilment. Suddenly Karl Walker too is a real person, without the mask of security, a troubled man.

Today, then, in the evening I shall go down to Frau Walker's room and ask her to tell me the end of her story, if one calls it the end ("If it hadn't been for that business with the baby carriage"). Today, as my own defenseless frame of mind, this unusual susceptibility to the lives of others, will assure, I shall understand that this story, whatever horrors it may contain, signifies love in its innermost recesses, that love which maintains the world.

But that evening Sabine arrived. Which Sabine? There are seven Sabines inside that one Sabine. No, probably more than seven, one can't claim to know the whole of her just because one has been working with her for a year and spent an occasional evening with her outside working hours. "The room brightens up when Fräulein Sabine comes in," that's the formula for one of the Sabines, I have heard it more than once, out of the head librarian's mouth, for instance. "But really, she's the most mysterious creature on God's earth"; that refers to another of the Sabines. Sabine the practical, Sabine the ruler—yes, she can rule all right, at her desk at the library above all; Sabine the high-spirited—but very few know of *her*. Still more rarely does one meet Sabine the timid, the fugitive. If one could see the whole of her one might call her Sabine the guest.

As for her past, here are a few outlines,

all that I know of it; only as much as one
learns from a friend, flashes of lightning
that give you a glimpse of the landscape, a
breath or two of changeless air. (So-called
"complete records" are a matter for the po-
lice or, as one would once have said, for the
family album.) Well, then: Sabine Berendson, daughter of a Jewish publisher and his
non-Jewish wife, born in 1928, in outward
appearance takes after her mother: tall, ash-
blond hair, blue eyes; in her character—but
how can I say, in her character she takes
after her father, when I have no other knowledge of that father than what I gathered
from Sabine's scanty account? She spoke of
this father, who lives at Cambridge, as one
speaks of the heroes of legends, to be more
precise, of legends about the saints. By peril-
ous ways, disguised as an Aryan, Sabine had
survived the Hitler regime; when no other
resort was left to them, her parents had
agreed on a merely formal separation, for
the sake of their daughter's future. "Till the
evil spell is broken," they had said, but then

the mother had died on an April day in 1945, died at a moment when dying had ceased to be a personal matter (engulfed with the rest, dug in with the rest), while Sabine was away on "compulsory foreign service"—that's what they called it then— leaving no news, no death certificate, no description of the grave and, strangely enough, no very deep impression on her daughter's memory. Her father had been able to flee the country at a moment when no other means of survival seemed possible for persons of his kind. One autumn evening in the year 1945—all unforgettable, day and hour, weather and color of the sky—she received news that he was alive; the British Commandant of the town had passed it on to her; it was like a second birth, *incipit vita nova*. But here and now Sabine was alone, very much alone, Sabine the guest.

The guest: a person who feels a deep kinship with the ephemeral things of this life and will never understand the meaning of goods and chattels, safety of bolt and lock.

There's the special way in which she hangs up her duffel coat on entering the room, as if making sure that she can take it down again without loss of time; there's the special way in which she follows the smoke of her cigarette with her eyes, blue cloud, adieu. ... To bring you a bunch of flowers is something that would occur to her easily, to bring you something more lasting, a cactus plant, say, never. And so in all things. She'll never take to the idea of a fine collection of phonograph records ("Oh, my dear fellow, there's your stock of canned goods again"), but she's always chasing the radio waves at night. ("Do you remember: tocktocktocktock; *hier ist London, hier ist London, hier ist London?*") Photographic feats she despises utterly: "Not for me," she says. "That is for people who have to hang on to time, who're afraid of losing their faces." Telephone calls, on the other hand, long conversations with long pauses, are something after her own heart. "Wonderful, how it makes words reach their right place, the only place

38

worthy of them, the wholly imaginary."
Which of these Sabines might be coming
today?

She came with her head in a cloud—
never disturb the other when his head is in a
cloud, that's an unwritten law of friendship
—took off her coat, asked for a cigarette,
and filled the kettle. Then she took the tea
from the shelf and set the table for us both;
it was like a silent ritual. For a moment,
three moments in all, just till the water
boiled, she made herself comfortable on the
couch. To be here, to be accepted and borne
up, three floors up, thirty floors up, as high
as love can—but without forgetting that
we're on our way, that this is only a way
station. A station lasting as long as a heartbeat, perhaps as long as a kiss. She looked
at me; Sabine the guest. And suddenly I
knew what it meant, and understood all at
once where Sabine belongs. She is part of
Frau Walker's story. I don't yet know the
place. (Really I must hear the end of that
story. Tonight, perhaps? No, not tonight.

39

This is Sabine's hour.) But what is her place in the story?

"Tell me, Sabine, where did you spend the summer of '42?"

"The summer of '42? I was at Offenbach, still at school. Fourth form, no, already the fifth. And then, the beginning of September, I came here."

"You came here?"

"Yes. My father urgently wanted us to get swallowed up in a large city, my mother and myself. He thought there'd be a better chance here, a better chance of getting me through it all unmolested, as he hoped. 'I tell you, we'll manage it after all,' he said a few times before the separation, looking at me in a way I can't describe. 'The very image of Germania,' he said. 'And once you've dropped the Berendson, I tell you, we'll manage it after all, you'll come through.' They had decided that we should be known by my mother's surname. Uncanny that: to give up one's name. One never knows what else one's giving up with it."

40

"But you must have known even then what the game was, and that it wasn't a 'game'?"

"Yes . . . and no. Yes, I suppose I understood. At first I wanted to say that everything was quite different at the time from what it seems like in retrospect. My father, you see, my father loved Germany. He'd fought in the First World War. My father . . . yes, that's what he's like: he simply doesn't know how to hate. In our house we lived as if we were on an island. My father wore the yellow star, but he wore it like a decoration. I've never seen Father angry, only silent. I'll tell you the story about Rebecca, then you'll understand what things were like at that time. And what Father was like. Rebecca—but I can't tell you the story in such a loud voice. Come a bit nearer—"

I sat down on the couch, Sabine put her arms round my neck and continued her story in a whisper, as if there were a stranger in the room who must not be allowed to overhear what she said. Perhaps that stran-

ger was Death, or the enemy, or the specter
of fear.

"Rebecca, then. At that time, at Offenbach, Rebecca was my friend, it was the
only time I really had a friend; on the whole
I'm not very good at keeping up friend-
ships, people always demand too much. Rebecca was the daughter of the cantor in the
synagogue, and she looked just like Rebecca
at the well, you can probably imagine what
that was like—you know: 'Both drink thou,
and I will also draw for thy camels.' She
was only a year older than I was, but really
she was years older, for she already had a
genuine life of her own. When the arrests
began, the cantor and his wife hid their
daughter, always sending her to a different
family; people could be trusted to keep a secret, it worked pretty well. A few times she
stayed with us too, we had long conversations before going to sleep, they were the
kind one doesn't easily forget. But then suddenly Rebecca had vanished. 'Where's Rebecca?' I asked them every day, morning,

noon and night; I knew: without Rebecca
the world was not the same. She's gone
away, my mother said, and it wasn't even
untrue. She *had* gone away, to Auschwitz,
I think, to the gas chamber—but my mother
said nothing about that. People should tell
the truth, but I don't blame them for not
telling me the whole truth then. 'Where's
Rebecca?' I remember asking. I was alone
in the room with my father and asked the
question for the twentieth, for the thirtieth
time: 'Where's Rebecca?' And my father replied, 'In you.' And that's all he said. It was
as if he wanted to give me time to—how
shall I put it—to spell it out; 'In you.' And
only after a little pause he added, 'One
doesn't lose people whom one loves so much.'
Then I understood, as far as one would at
thirteen or fourteen, and I remember that I
kissed his hand. He took me in his arms. By
that time he'd already made up his mind
about the separation, and when I think of
that moment now, I know that all this was

43

already contained in the way he looked at me and consoled me, and in his words. He was already living like a fugitive; he worked in a small back room now, the main office was occupied by his successors. Even at home we saw next to nothing of him, he crept into his own house late at night. But what his look meant to tell me that day was: 'I shan't lose you either.' "

"I shan't lose you either." Sabine was silent. There was nothing more to be said about Offenbach and nothing more about her father. History was extinguished, as a candle is extinguished; the present revealed its face, a holy and mighty face. "If only it would stay like that"; these are simple words, the simplest of all. We both thought them, and each of us knew that the other was thinking them. But we did not say them.

"Another cigarette, if you don't mind. And let's have some music; couldn't you look for something good?" I switched on the radio and let the dial travel from name to name; Europe's transmitters released their flow of gurgling soapsuds, indigestible all of it; but here—stop—and Sabine too cried "Stop!"—this was music, truly perfect nocturnal music, Locatelli or Cimarosa. "What is it, Sabine? It isn't Mozart, it must be earlier, less encumbered."

"Oh, don't worry about it, my dear. No need to stick labels on it. Let's just be glad it's there at all, that it is as it is and that there's a place for it in the world, a healthy place among all the scabs and pus. It won't last us very long, but at least it exists."

Who knows Sabine? She had turned toward the window and only glanced at me for a moment between two gulps of air that were almost sighs. Then she came up to me, kissed me once more, but only as in parting, and said, "Did you know you've got my father's eyes? Another reason for coming to see you from time to time." And then, in a different tone of voice: "Excuse this nonsense, just one feminine tear and a half. Too

45

silly of me. What do you say to a short walk?"

"A good idea, Sabine. Let's go."

We were standing in the hallway, I was looking for my key, when the door was opened from the outside; Frau Walker had come home. We said good evening; I wondered whether I ought to introduce Sabine, it was the first opportunity and it seemed suitable enough. Frau Walker looked up at Sabine, something seemed to be going on in her face, and she said, "Excuse me, miss, and you too, sir, must excuse me, but— you're Sabine Berendson, aren't you?"

"Yes." The "yes" was almost a gasp.

"And your father?"

"My father?" (This is even weirder than I thought). "My father lives in England— at Cambridge . . . "

46

"Then your father's alive. I'm so happy to hear it."

"But—"

We had no chance to ask further questions. What we saw now was that face with curtains drawn which I knew from Tuesday last, and really I had known it long before that Tuesday evening. At a face like that one doesn't fire questions. "How do you come to know me? I don't think we've ever met. And how do you come to know my father?" Such questions may present themselves. But no question is permitted.

Meanwhile Frau Walker had unlocked her glass door. "Good night," she said, nodding at us, and added, "Have a good time together." We liked the sound of this "together." The special sound it has for two people who are seeking their way. We walked out into a fine evening rain and felt as if Frau Walker's "together" were keeping watch over us.

"How extraordinary!" It was I who broke

the silence. "I really don't know what to say. That it makes me believe in clairvoyance is the least of it. There you stand for a moment on the threshold, in the dimness of the hallway light, and a strange woman tells you you're Sabine Berendson. And how did she find out anything about your father?"

"That's the most incomprehensible thing of all. True, my father's been here once or twice, years ago, for interviews with publishers, I think, for a day or two at a time. He liked the town, that I know, and the countryside too, and that may be why he chose to send us here of all places, but how on earth could he have run into Frau Walker?"

"And then she said: 'You're Sabine Berendson, aren't you?'"

"Of course my face may not be altogether unknown to her. If someone so openly displays one's photograph on his chest of drawers, as you do, then the landlady, who most probably tidies up your room from time to time, may recognize that face, possibly even

48

in the hallway at night. But my father's name—how does she come to know his name? You must find out. No, *I* must find it out. I shall write to my father."

WHY DID IT OCCUR TO ME THAT THERE was a letter for me in the box by the staircase, now, at this late hour? The light in the hallway had gone out at the moment I withdrew my key from the front-door latch, after returning from my walk with Sabine. I had climbed my three flights of stairs in the dark, put everything back in its place—not without great sadness, as usual—and made up my couch for the night. Could it be that there was a letter for me in the box downstairs?

For a time one struggles against inertia, one's reluctance to climb the stairs again, and calls on reason to support it by arguing that no one delivers letters at such a late hour, but suddenly one does find oneself on the stairs, ready to pursue the mirage.

It is not a mirage. There *is* a letter. A letter with no stamps and no sender's address. I did not know the hand that had written my two names on the envelope, but before I had opened it, I knew: this is a letter from Frau Walker.

Was I surprised? By the fact that she had written to me? By the handwriting itself, the freedom and assurance of its sweep? No, I was not surprised. I had been surprised when I heard myself saying "now," that somehow challenging "now" of the other night; for willingly and consciously I had entered the shaft whose name is: the Unheard-of, the Unpredictable. Now it was not for me to wonder at anything that might happen.

This is her letter:

Dear Sir: Since you came to see me everything that had been left in the dark for years has been stirred up again. There was a time when I could not face these things, even in thought. But now it seems almost a good thing that I've been forced to face them again, and I want to tell you more about them; in writing this is a little easier than by word of mouth. For when I sit facing the sheet of paper, I have time to wait for them to come again, stay for a while and move on —I mean the people of those years—and I think to myself: as long as I write about them and as long as you read about them, tomorrow or the day after, these people are really with us again. Of course I know that it won't be much of a letter.

I've already told you that I knew next to nothing about the Jews. It was only by having all this wretched business thrown at me every Friday evening that I found out about them. And I understood where a decent person belongs, and discovered what a decent person must do. Or rather I soon knew what one ought to have done, what was the proper thing to have done. But, then, we all failed to do this proper thing. At the very most, if

all went well, we threw a little drop of water
into a roaring fire. Sometimes a soldier on
leave gave you a meat coupon or two, and
those you then shared out on a Friday evening, so that one or another of them got a
little snippet more than the tiny amount to
which he was entitled by the card. Those
ration cards: if you had to handle them week
after week, you learned to read them like a
book. For instance, there might be a card
that differed from the others in giving the
owner a little supplement, a handful of bar-
ley, it might be, or a quarter pound of bread
—but how dearly they had to pay for such
beggar's fare. The man entitled to it was
forced to work in an arms factory, happily
employed in producing munitions. And what
were those used for? For the "fateful com-
bat," as they called it; but also for the mass
executions over there in the East. And the
man who produced cartridges here knew it
well enough. Or else I was handed two children's ration cards across the counter. But
I didn't see the cards with all their blank

spaces, what I saw was the children themselves and their outlawed lives: each of them
standing alone in his back yard, not under-
standing why his playmates act like a lot of
strangers. "Come over and play with me!"
And the other voice replies, "My mother
said I mustn't play with you any more. German boys don't play with a Jew-boy, she
said." One day someone's left a foul drawing
on a school desk and a word goes round the
class, an insulting word; "shickse," they say,
children are cruel, and the *Stürmer* on the
notice board has long ago made sure that
even the youngest are well-informed.

And then there's the old man who doesn't
understand at all. It takes him a long time
to find his ration card in his pocket, and
longer to spread it out on the counter. He
seems astonished all the time, as he looks
round with a half-smile, but this half-smile
cuts into your soul. "Germans—goot people, Germans—not bat," he says to me, in
the accent and intonation of Czenstochau in

Poland; I feel a lump in my throat, and I
don't say what I'm thinking: Germans bad.

Now, sir, don't say: that Frau Walker is
delirious. I'm not delirious, though I am
seeing things. I can see them standing in
front of my counter, eight or ten or twelve
of them at a time. Women, children, and old
men—the younger men have become very
rare; I get to know their names and read
their faces; whether I read them aright, I
can't say, but I suppose you can learn anything if you practice long enough. "Well,
what are they like, then, your Friday night
Jews?" someone would ask from time to
time. "Just an alien mob, aren't they? And
sinister? And unkempt?"

Alien? Yes, they feel alien enough. And
unkempt. But let anyone try to keep clean
without enough soap, without washing facili-
ties, without textiles, without new leather.
And sinister? No, not sinister, only sad, very
sad. I'm reminded of the children, the first
two, who spent half an hour in my sitting
room, the selfsame room in which we talked

the other night. I'd noticed that two mothers
had other shopping to do elsewhere and that
their children were almost too tired to go with
them. "The children can wait here till you
come back," I'd said to the two women,
opening the door to this small room. "You
sit down here like good girls," I said to them,
and it was quite a while before I could see
to them again, for I was kept pretty busy
trying to serve everyone, at least for the first
few months. After that—but I'll come to
that later. At last I had a free moment and
went in to see what the children were doing.
There they were, still sitting together on a
single chair, and it was obvious that they
hadn't stirred from their places. I cut up
part of a wartime cake, we ran to cake of a
sort from time to time; they looked at me
incredulously when I offered them the plate:
"Share it between you!" Their mothers came
back and called the children; they wouldn't
shake hands with me, but the two mothers
gave me a long look; almost hostile, I
thought, this look was—but what do we

know àbout such things? Whether they were alien to me, people had asked me, those Friday evening Jews. (But excuse me, sir, I've already written about that; you must understand that it isn't easy for me to keep to one thread.) Well, they were alien to me; but when people spoke with so much commiseration and mistrust about "my Jews," I should have liked to answer back, "That's right, they're my Jews."

I've already told you about those other visitors who would arrive so suddenly from time to time. As long as they were there, none of my customers would say anything that wasn't absolutely necessary, but there were Fridays when no patrol came our way, and then they'd talk to me. I never asked them to talk, but neither did I turn a deaf ear when they did talk. All I knew was that they needed someone who'd listen to them. Even if he couldn't do anything to help them.

That's how it was at the start. But then came that business with the wrapping paper. Frau M. — I still know her name, but I got

58

so used to abbreviations, I'll put one here
if you don't mind—Frau M. was one of the
most refined of my Friday evening customers, and at the same time she was one of the
bluntest, if you can say any of them was
blunt. When most of these customers were
already talking to me quite openly, she never
said a word that could be left unsaid. In fact
I hardly knew the sound of her voice—till
the day when she quite unexpectedly addressed me, and came out with a whole sentence. "My sister-in-law is coming later,"
she said. "She'll collect my ration. Keep it
for her, please, and"—she hesitated—"and
wrap up the meat in this," pulling a piece
of gray wrapping paper out of her handbag.
I wanted to reply, "Don't trouble yourself,
there's no need—there's no shortage of wrapping paper yet," but she said, "Please!" And
this "Please!" was so severe that I could
only nod my head and do what she asked.
Her sister-in-law never came that day, and
the gray paper was still on the counter when
I closed the shop. I picked it up and was

just about to wrap up the meat in it, as
Frau M. had asked me to do, when I dis-
covered a pencilled note on the gray paper.
It read: "Sigi is gone, Theresienstadt, Block
XVII, will you write to him—Love M."

Did I mention that on her way out Frau
M. had turned her head and said "Many
thanks," just those two words, loud and dis-
tinct?

On the following Friday—I was worried
about this business—the sister-in-law appeared. I had to be very careful that day, as
the visitors had come, and somehow I was
more conscious than usual of being under
observation; I dare say it was a kind of
premonition. I took advantage of a moment
when the SS Men were talking to each other
to say: "Your sister-in-law left her ration
behind last time she was here. She asked me
to keep it for you. Do you think Frau M.
herself will be coming today? If not, I could
let you have something else as well. I've
made a note of the amount." If only those
young fellows don't get interested in us, I

thought, and I felt my heart throb in my
throat. "Frau M. doesn't need her ration any
more," her sister-in-law said very quickly;
a slight motion of her hand toward her
throat told me everything. That was the kind
of language we used in those days. I knew
at once: they've taken the husband away, the
wife scribbles a brief note to inform her sis-
ter that the man has been "transported," and
then she goes off and does away with herself.
Can I be sure the overseers haven't noticed
this motion of the woman's hand? They have
not, thank God! They go to the door and
take their leave in the terms they think fitting. "Perish Judea!" they bawl out, and
then, "Heil Hitler!"

Now it strikes me how curious it was that
the others hardly talked among themselves,
as if the general terror had taken hold of
them too and estranged one from another.
And at times it really looked like that, as if
they distrusted one another. For a time I
even suspected that it was one of themselves
who had been partly responsible for having

61

the rabbi "transported." You see, sir, from that place behind the counter one really had a good view of the world in those days, I mean the real world outside in which all things can happen, the best and the worst. That Dr. Ehrenreich must have known too that all things are possible, that you can't even rely on being safe with your own people, but of course he couldn't have acted otherwise than he did.

I stopped here for a while, to rest my hand. I looked out of the window, and that recalled the war nights. That's how one used to stand in the dark, listening up into the sky, listening for the planes at night. Then I started rereading these last pages myself, and I notice that I haven't told you anything about that rabbi yet; as I said, you must excuse me if this story reads like a crazy jumble of events—as far as I'm concerned, Rabbi Ehrenreich was present again all the time I was writing.

I've already told you how I wondered why they hardly spoke to one another; and

the first reason why I took notice of the
rabbi was just that they always hailed him
when he came in and spoke to him, even if
they spoke to no one else. I should never
have known he was a rabbi, for in appearance—at least in dress—he didn't differ from
other old men. The shopping net he carried
was usually heavy by the time he came to
the shop. He had to buy all the rations for
seven or eight people, every time. What did
he look like? He looked like—well, at the
time I didn't know, as I hadn't yet started
reading the Bible properly, I only knew it
suddenly when I came to read the Book of
Jeremiah; that's what he looked like, the
prophet Jeremiah himself. Usually he came
on the stroke of six. One day, I remember,
the bell of St. Peter's—there was only one
bell left in the clocktower at that time—had
just been rung, and after the ringing there
was real silence for a few moments. Then
the rabbi spoke one word in a loud voice. I
heard the sound clearly, but couldn't understand. Later I learned that word. He had

said "Shalom," and when he said it all the
people in the shop stood quite motionless.
Then he said other words, and I knew it
must be a prayer or a text from the Bible,
for everyone took part in silence. This had become their synagogue now. I kept very quiet
and put the knife away. (My only fear was
that the black visitors might come just at
that moment; this would mean trouble.)
And then suddenly I noticed one customer
looking at the rabbi with an evil, a really
vicious glance. It was a young fellow who
rarely came here, since his mother did most
of the shopping. He stepped up to the counter and, in the midst of that silence, said
to me in a very loud voice, "How much do
I owe you?" I named the sum as quietly as
possible but he put the coins on the tray
one by one, taking care to produce a loud
noise with each, and then said at the top of
his voice, "Good evening to you, then," and
left the shop. The other customers never
turned to look at him, the service went on.
But I thought to myself: so that's how it is,

with them as well as with us; this is the com-
munity, but that young fellow is no longer
with it. But what a good thing the black men
didn't come today, I thought again.

A week later—everything was the same,
only the vicious boy's mother had come in
his place and a few of the other customers
were different ones—the rabbi spoke the
same words, and I myself felt I was taking
part in this strange service of which I didn't
understand a word; so I forgot my sentry
duty—no one had commanded me to be a
sentry, but one has to keep some sort of
watch over people praying as they flee. The
door suddenly opened, at the very moment
when the rabbi was extending his arm in
blessing; his congregation, still in a sort of
trance, couldn't move back quick enough
into the everyday world—and the intruders
were already in the shop, no less than four
of them, too. The leader, a great giant of a
man, called out, "Heil Hitler! What's going on in this place? D'you think this is a
church or a Jews' brothel or something?"

And he went straight up to the rabbi with a threatening gesture.

"Hey, Yid, I'm talking to you!"

And I remember every word of the rest.

"My name is Dr. Ehrenreich," said the rabbi. (That's when it struck me that he looked like a prophet.)

"A Yid is what you are," this giant Goliath shouted, "a filthy bastard of a Jew. What do you think you were doing just now?"

"I was praying."

"That won't get you a sausage to stuff into your belly."

"It isn't for sausages I pray, but for human beings."

"Your lot certainly need to."

"We all need to."

"There's no accounting for tastes. I wouldn't like to be in your dirty mouth, Yid."

"It is not God's will that you should perish."

There was a great silence now, a terrible silence, and all looked on, my customers and

66

the other's companions; it seemed to me that the men in black uniforms were even more startled than those who had been roused from their prayers.

David and Goliath—that's how I thought of them now. And I wondered if the story would really be allowed to end differently in this case. Was it really possible that it should end in this way: that the small and venerable man would be dragged out by his beard and transported, sir, never again to be heard of or seen?

You can imagine the feelings with which I waited for the following Friday night. Some days I considered whether I should report those men, for breaking the peace in a private dwelling, perhaps, but there was not the slightest hope that justice would be done. There was no longer such a thing as justice. Yet at times a delay occurred in the workings of injustice itself; and it is to such delays that many of us owe our lives. The following Friday passed without a visit from the intruders; and quite a number of other

Fridays passed quietly enough. Those weeks
—I've given a great deal of thought to them
since—were no less strange for that. For
after this incident my Friday customers began to talk differently among themselves. It
was just as if this calamity had loosened all
their tongues. And—strange or not strange,
I don't know—they began to speak to me
too in a different way, different from the
first months, I mean. The little living room
that had once harbored the two children was
never empty now, and it wasn't only on Fridays that we met there. That was about the
time, too, when the Hebrew book came my
way, the one you found on my bookshelf. A
doctor's wife brought it for me, as a parting
gift, and you know what sort of a parting
that was. It was a pretty risky game I was
playing then, there's no doubt about it. And
I needn't tell you that it wasn't only a game.

Still another new sheet. I know I'm asking a lot of you, sir, and my handwriting
isn't quite what it used to be, as my sight has
never quite recovered from the effect of that

fire; but, I told you right at the start the
other day, it was the business with the baby
carriage that brought everything to a head,
and that's something I shouldn't be able to
talk about if you were sitting just in front
of me here.

It was the sixteenth of October; you know
the date because it was the day the Museum
Library was destroyed, and it was a Friday.
Everything was the same as ever, I stood
behind the counter, my customers handed me
their ration cards, trustingly now and without fear; they had ceased to pray in the shop
since the rabbi's transportation, but sometimes I was the one who said "Shalom" instead of the usual greeting for now I knew
well what the word means, and the person
addressed would often reply, "Shalom."
That was our Sabbath in the butcher's shop.
. . . I heard a car draw up; its door was shut
with a bang, so that I just had time to call
out "Careful!" before Goliath was in the
shop. He had been followed by a feeble little
fellow stuck into a uniform that didn't seem

to belong to him. I went on with my work as
if I hadn't noticed them at all, but I saw at
once that the giant had been promoted to a
higher rank since his last visit; one had
learned to pay attention to such things. It
was clear that they'd lost no time in reward-
ing him for his recent feat. By the peculiar
fixed gaze he directed at different parts of
the shop I could see that he'd been drinking.
He lit a cigarette and, after drawing at it,
pushed the burning end into an old man's
face; the action was so sudden that the first
I knew of it was the victim's cry of pain.
Now things are going to get bad, I thought,
very bad indeed. And I knew at once: I
would not be silent in this case. The time for
silence was past.

"Smoking is prohibited here by law," I
said, stressing the word "law." Our Goliath
turned his eyes on me, as if he'd just grown
aware of my presence, then he read the
printed notice which I'd indicated with a
jerk of my head, and to my surprise he trod
out the cigarette, though he'd only just be-

gun to smoke it, but with an evil smile on
his face. He turned to the customer nearest
to him—it was a former judge, long retired.
"Are you quite sure you couldn't still get
away?" I'd asked him recently, and he'd an-
swered: "No, I can't get away any more,
I'm too old; and I don't want to either, my
gravestone's waiting for me here." Now I
saw the big fellow knock the package of
meat out of his hand. "Yid!" he called out,
"you'd better not eat too much, or you'll get
too heavy for your ascension. You're off on
the fifteenth—whiz-bang, you'll fly through
the air with the greatest of ease!"

Everyone looked at Goliath. Only two
or three customers pretended they hadn't
heard, and one of them went up to me to
state his order. I couldn't attend to him at
once, for I had to see to Frau Zalewsky. She
had put her bag on the floor and stood trem-
bling all over. She was a musician's wife and
was expecting a baby any day now. I knew
quite a bit about her. She'd had the effron-
tery to apply for the "Supplementary Ra-

tion for Expectant Mothers" in the fourth
month of her pregnancy, about a half-pint
of milk and a few ounces of sugar and flour.
Her application had been returned with this
statement: "What a Jew's bastard needs is
abortion. Apply to the Health Department,
Section D." She preserved this document in
her handbag and had once shown it to me. I
read it, looked carefully at the stamp and sig-
nature, even making a mental note of the
typist's initials: if one could dictate a sentence like that one to a secretary, there
wasn't much one couldn't do. "Frau Zalewsky!" I said now. "Don't worry," she replied,
deathly pale, "I'll feel better in a moment."
I went back to the customer who—quite un-
moved, it seemed—repeated his order. The
big fellow started again: "Whiz-bang, whiz-
bang, you'll fly through the air with the
greatest of ease. . . ." It looked as if he was
about to perform some sort of war dance,
when his puny, scraggy companion, himself
a little David now, took one pace toward the
towering great fellow, jumped to attention

and said in a very quiet voice, "Untersturmführer, please remember you're on duty."

Goliath opened his eyes wide and shot out
one arm. It seemed incredible to him that
anyone should dare to put him in his place.
And now he erupted: "That's a lot of hog-
wash! Why, I'm doing them a real favor—
don't you start making trouble, Beck, just
keep your shirt on, will you—a real favor,
I say, breaking it to them gradually—real
bedside manner and all—just giving them a
delicate hint that they'll soon be going up
the chimney. Can't you see, Beck, that Sarah
over there with the big belly, she's just
beaming with gratitude—aren't you, Sarah?
—for telling her she needn't worry any more
about the baby's diapers, those dear little
shitty diapers—"

"Untersturmführer!" the young man
called out again, and it sounded almost as if
he was pleading; then he took hold of his
superior's arm.

"Hands off, damn you!" he yelled, in a
drunken rage, but at the same time made for

73

the door with long unsteady steps. When he'd followed him to the door, the little fellow turned around and called out to me, "You'll keep your mouth shut!" I nodded. Why shouldn't I keep quiet, when the stones themselves would speak?

I continued my work in silence, and no one there said another word that evening. I cut the week's coupons out of the cards and handed the goods across the counter. It came into my head—and even now, after many years, I wonder what made me do it— to give each customer much more than his proper ration. All I remember is that when they'd all gone, and I realized I'd most probably never be able to make up for this loss, I felt relieved and almost cheerful. I could still hear those dreadful words re-echo round the shop, but when I locked the door behind the last customer, I felt as if the whole burden had already been lifted from my shoulders.

An hour had gone by, I was sitting in my room and doing some sewing, when I heard a faint knock at my window. I got up to open the door. I'm not very brave, sir. I was very frightened. It was no longer as I'd thought before, I mean about the burden having been lifted from my shoulders. The burden was still there, as heavy as ever. It was Frau Zalewsky, the musician's wife, who'd come to see me. "Open the door for a moment, please," she said. I unlocked it at once. Frau Zalewsky had stepped back for a moment into the dark side passage and now returned, pushing something toward the door. It was a baby carriage. She pushed it straight through the outer door and into the room, the same room in which I'm writing this down. The baby carriage stood in the very place where you were sitting the other night; and, as far as I'm concerned, it's still standing there. . . .

"Do take a seat, Frau Zalewsky," I said; she sat down, in the awkward way a woman sits down in her last weeks of pregnancy. Then she began: "It's true—it's true what that man said."

"The one who was drunk, you mean?" I wanted it to sound like a doubt, but I'd only to listen to my own voice to know that I'd said it without conviction. The world has become so bad that only the very worst is true.

"Yes, that one," the woman confirmed. "The rabbi once said: 'God created wine to loosen the tongues of fools, that they may speak the truth unto those that seek truth.' "

And then: silence. I kept my eyes lowered. Then the woman's voice again: "I've brought you that baby carriage. You've been good to me all this time. I thought, maybe you'll need it one day, Frau Walker, later, I mean." And again: silence. Then: "I must go now. Thank you again for everything. Where shall we put it?"

"Oh, just leave it where it is, thank you." That's all I could think of saying.

At the front door Frau Zalewsky turned her head once more; it was quite dark now and I could hardly see her, but I heard her voice and thought to myself: a true child of Rabbi Ehrenreich, that's what she's like—

76

no, a true descendant of the ancient proph-
ets. The sky was full of autumn stars that
night. The last words I heard her say—and
one doesn't forget such words—were so
faint, they sounded far away; very softly,
she said: "And the word of the Lord came
unto Abram, saying: Look now toward
heaven, and tell the stars, if thou be able to
number them: and he said unto him, So shall
thy . . . "

I don't know whether she said any more;
the night seemed to swallow her words, and
she was already on her way. I went back to
the room and stared at the baby carriage. I
fetched the official sheets for the coupons
and started sticking them on. And the carriage stood just in front of me. It wasn't
empty; there was a blanket inside, a pillow
and some baby clothes. When it has come to
this, when a woman expecting her first child
has to give away the baby carriage because
the death sentence has been pronounced over
her unborn child without cause, when that
can happen the world can never be right

again. You just can't restore the balance. And really there's no remedy left, except one: to clear up thoroughly—with fire.

I don't remember very much more about that night. We hadn't much energy left by the end of the day, at that stage of the war, and it's quite likely that I simply dropped off to sleep over those coupons. They got burned too in the fire, and you can imagine how much trouble that caused me later. I dare say I still heard the air raid warnings, but probably took them for something quite different. Why I didn't get up when it all started, that's something I don't know till this day. And then it all took the course which it had to take; I think you know what that course was.

Now it's almost dawn, sir, and I've just finished rereading this letter once more. Now I must end by thanking you very much for hearing my story out.

Yours sincerely,
Margarete Walker.

No, I did not know what had happened after that. I knew nothing at all about it.

Whether she, Frau Walker, surprised by the sirens and the British bombers (it was the very raid that is commemorated on the stone tablet to be found in the reconstructed Museum Library), saw fit to abandon all this, all her possessions, the house and herself to the alien fire, believing, perhaps, that one individual at least must crawl into the fiery furnace and take no thought for safety —or whether she was simply tired out, too tired to return to a world in which a mother has to part with her unborn baby's carriage —this question remains open, and I for one am not likely ever to find out the truth. I shall never ask anyone about it; one does not ask questions about such things. Besides, this letter and its message are sufficient in themselves.

Such is the world. Such is the monstrous face of Power. Such are the mauled and mangled lives of those who have passed through the great mincing machine of the

age. And such is the infinitesimal, the mar-
vellous possibility of man. One can hand
over a piece of wrapping paper and conceal
a message inside it. One can offer slices of
cake to a couple of children. And, at the
very end, one can take in a baby carriage—
all these things one can do. An hour's trust
and safety, a breath of peace. But no blos-
soming avenue of this world grants a radi-
ance as bright as that light which penetrated
through a chink in the door of the Jews'
butcher, who stored up cubes of meat extract
and often enough had nothing better to offer
her customers than bits of tough beef full of
bones and gristle.

SABINE TELEPHONED. NINE DAYS HAD passed since our conversation that night and we'd hardly seen each other since: she'd been to Hanover on business and I'd only just been able to hand her Frau Walker's long letter before the train moved off. Now —soon after the end of our office hours— she called me up. From the voice alone I could tell that it wasn't any of the Sabines I knew.

"My father has written."

"Oh. I suppose he didn't mention Frau Walker?"

"He mentioned nothing else. You must come to see me. Soon. At once. Tonight. It's important."

I went. Sabine's father's letter lay on the table beside Frau Walker's letter. They lay on the table like omens, separate omens that will nevertheless combine, because one keeps watch over the other. Who will combine them?

"Everything after the first sheet," Sabine said.

"You read it to me."

"No." It was almost a shriek. "I can't. One can't read that kind of letter to *anyone.*"

" . . . and never thought, my dear, that I should ever have to tell you directly about those events. True, I always knew I mustn't depart from this life without leaving an account of them. But this account was to be kept locked up indefinitely, a testament, as it were. But I suppose I'd better tell you now what you don't know: that during the summer months of 1942 I returned for a few weeks to your immediate vicinity, so that in fact I saw you there once or more than once every day. So I know everything about your way of life in those days, even your way to school in that town. I was there

before eight o'clock in the morning and soon
after noon, when you went home for lunch.
I know every dress you wore in those days.
I saw you wear the embroidered blouse
which I'd once brought back for your mother
from Dalmatia, and I saw my child turn
into a young lady, a little more so each day.
I saw your face and the faces of the girl
friends who went home with you. Sometimes
I heard you laugh. Often enough I stood
quite close to you, but I never yielded to the
temptation to speak to you again. I was
aware of the confusion this would bring into
your life and your mother's life, and so I
desisted, much as I should have liked you to
know I was there. For homesickness was
just beginning to consume me. There are
twenty-four hours in the day, and in every
one of those hours it can make itself felt.
It's six o'clock in the morning, and Sabine
is getting up. It's noon, and Sabine is start-
ing her lunch. It's getting dark and Sabine
will soon go to bed. It's nighttime, and Sabine wakes up. It's the hour for prayer, and

Sabine does not join me in prayer. I'm listening to music, and Sabine doesn't hear it. A tree is in leaf, and Sabine doesn't see it. That's how it was.

Like all of us, I had to get my meat ration at Frau Walker's; and during my last week in Germany I twice had the chance to talk to her after closing time. On the second of those two evenings I showed her the photographs I carried in my wallet. This isn't the moment to speak about Frau Walker, or rather about the matters we discussed on those two occasions. She looked at your photographs; you can see how intently she looked at them from the fact that she recognized you in the hallway on your way out with Dr. S. (to whom I send my best wishes). There was a place for us all in her gaze.

Then came the third evening, my last in that town, it was the sixteenth of October— I remember the date because on the morning of the seventeenth I received the great news, the express letter from Sweden that

informed me of the unexpected reprieve of
which you know. I was staying with the G's.,
quite close to Walker, the butcher's. There
was an air-raid alarm that night and at first
I stayed in my room, as usual. If only out
of consideration for the G's., I never made
use of the shelter in the cellar of the house,
and till then we'd got off lightly. But that
night they meant business. I heard the
bombs come down not many streets away
and suddenly thought of the public shelter
on the other side of the road. I hurried there
without dressing, but turned back again on
the stairs to get my overcoat. Often since
I've had occasion to reflect how very different that night would have been if I hadn't
gone back to get my coat. I dare say I should
have reached the shelter unhurt and perhaps
even got back safely to my room, for neither
the shelter nor our house received a direct
hit that night. As it was, I wore my coat
and, on it, the yellow star; the air-raid
warden in the shelter noticed it at once, at
the entrance, and forbade me to come in. It

was a bad moment, a moment I don't want to recall. As I turned back into the street I found it lit up by a great blaze, was met by smoke and the smell of burning, and decided to look for the fire—why, I don't know and shall never know. The anti-aircraft guns were in action and I heard the hum of foreign planes. I ran down the street and remember saying to myself, 'Of course!' when, turning the corner, I found that it was the Walkers' house that was blazing and pouring acrid smoke into the street. The top floor was on fire; the two lower ones, as far as one could see anything through the smoke, were still intact. But at the moment I came to the garden gate another bomb hit the house. I fell on my face and felt a violent blow on my chin; blood was trickling out of my mouth, but it didn't hurt, only my eyes smarted with the heat and smoke. You know I'm hardly an acrobat—but suddenly I was up on the window sill of the ground floor sitting room; all I know was that there was something I must

86

save in the Walkers' house. The last blast
had splintered the windowpanes. I saw—in
a cloud of fire—I saw Frau Walker sitting
at her table, called out to her but got no answer. I leaped into the room, rushed to the
door and opened it, when more fire broke in
from the hall. I seized her arm—she was
half-unconscious—risked the five or six
yards to the front door, found the key in
the lock—thank heaven—managed to turn it
and got her out. I was only slightly hurt,
but the woman's face looked ghastly in the
glow of the fire. Some fifty or sixty paces
away—as far as I could drag her, for she
could hardly be said to have walked—I laid
her on a bench and covered her with my
overcoat, having torn off part of her half-
smouldering skirt just in time. The bench, I
found, belonged to the next house but one;
it was safe enough for the moment. I'd long
ago made a mental note of the fire alarm in
our street and I found it quickly, broke the
glass and heard the sirens begin to wail. All
at once it struck me: on the overcoat cover-

ing Frau Walker there was that star, the yellow star. I hurried back and quickly ripped it off. Frau Walker opened her eyes; she recognized me now, smiled for a moment, but then said very softly and gravely, 'He has not accepted it.' 'Accepted what?' 'The burnt offering. God has not accepted it.'

Those were almost the last words I heard spoken in German, but I needn't tell you, Sabine, that I felt little desire to hear any others. The fire engine was on its way. They'd find the injured woman; my work was done.

I returned to my lodgings. Early next morning the Swedish courier arrived—Dr. G. had directed him—and gave me the letter that meant I was saved."

"No regards to Frau Walker," I said, as I pushed the letter over to Sabine; "that's strange."

"Yes, it is strange. But I suppose formalities hardly apply in such a case."

To CONCLUDE, THEN. BUT THIS IS ONE OF those ingenuities of life of which we say that they are both foolish and incomprehensible. A man goes on a journey for professional reasons, as he is sometimes obliged to do on account of an ancient manuscript he has never seen, and as he unpacks his briefcase at night in the hotel he happens to glance at a sheet of newspaper. At home he had taken a newspaper from the stack without looking, one of many newspapers mouldering in the junk room of the Walkers' house; now he is tired, distraught and only glad that he can bolt the door of his hotel bedroom and that his travelling flask of brandy isn't quite empty yet. So he spreads out the sheet of newspaper and lets his

glance wander over the short advertisements
column. "Walker," his eyes read, and he begins to take notice. "Walker" it is, no mis-
take.

And I read that Karl Walker, the
butcher, announces the re-opening of his
shop. I look for the date and see that the
paper is seven months old. "High Quality
Meat and Poultry. Specialists in Black
Pudding," it says. And in the margin, curiously lost in that place, a Bible reference,
II Moses 3:2. Like an afterthought added
in haste, it looked on that page, or as if in-
serted in the wrong place by a careless
printer. For what was a Bible reference doing here? You can understand the inclusion
of a Bible reference in the obituary notice
of a Christian, but what is the connection
between black pudding and II Moses 3?

The reference: a librarian should know
that the Moses story begins in the book of
Exodus and, if he knows his Bible, he will
remember that the third chapter relates how
Moses was called. But what is the passage

itself and what, if the reference is really not an accident, does it signify here?

It is a quarter to ten at night. Shall I trouble the hotel management for a Bible? I'm afraid they can provide anything rather than a Bible. I lift the receiver and ask the telephone exchange of the hotel to connect me with one of the parish offices in the town. It is Friday night (Frau Walker's evening, it occurs to me for a moment), and a quarter to ten, so it wouldn't be too importunate of me to telephone at this hour. The pastor will receive the call in his house, for he'll be working at his Sunday sermon at home, and that means his Bible won't be far away.

"What can I do for you?"

I state my name and my request. A Bible text is what I require.

"One moment, please." The pastor's voice is calm and betrays little astonishment. "Yes, here it is. The passage in question reads: ' . . . and he looked, and, behold, the bush burned with fire, and the bush was not consumed.' "

91

"And the bush was not consumed." I understood; it was a question, long ago posed in silence, and an answer, slowly grasped.

The question: whether there is one who can balance the terrible guilt of the age against the wild self-immolation of a butcher's wife, against this readiness to crawl into the fiery furnace.

But one who could draw up this balance will say that he "desires not sacrifice," that he "delights not in burnt offering" nor in "the peace offerings of your fat beasts," but only in a broken spirit and a contrite heart. And would say—and this is the answer—that all of them, even he who shares the knowledge of it, Sabine, too, so curiously interwoven with it, and Sabine's father, who saved and was saved, have been retained for further service. True, in the burn on the woman's face that sign will remain, the sign that must not be interpreted otherwise than as a sign of love, of that love which maintains the world. . . .

"Is there anything else I can do?"

I'd forgotten that I still held the receiver in my hand. All I heard was a vague noise.

"I beg your pardon?"

"Is there anything else I can do?"

"Anything else? No. Nothing else. Thank you. Thank you very much. Good night."